First edition

Written by: Karl Agapuu

Cover art by: Siim Pukk

www.agapuu.com

ISBN: 9798789046838

About the Author

KARL AGAPUU was born in a small fishing village of 20 people in Estonia. He is the only child of a truck driver father and a cashier mother. After high school he attended University of Tartu Pärnu College in Entrepreneurship and project manegement, but dropping out in year two, due to the belief that entrepreneurs are made in the ring, not behind a school desk.

Shortly after joining the workforce as a cashier, he started writing short stories and screenplays in hopes of one day working on something big in the City of Angels.

www.agapuu.com

Author's Note

This was my first ever attempt at writing fiction back in 2016. Back then I had no ambition of becoming a writer. I knew I wanted to do something in the film industry, but realizing I have no experience or even seen a film set, I had to start from somewhere. Deep down, there has always been hidden a dream of writing and starring in your own film like one of my idols Stallone. But again, no experience would be the obstacle. So that's when I started to experiemtn with short stories to work myself up to a full length feature film script. Short stories have been a detrimental factor in my career and I always enjoy writing them.

Work: #1

Written: April 2016

Age: 22

Published: December 23rd 2021

"Fishing can't be this fucking difficult!" yelled Mholda at the lake as he reeled in another round of seaweed, barely holding on to his makeshift rod made of a willow branch and thin old rope he had found from a nearby cavern. "There's a line, a rod and a hook. Three components, you can't fuck it up!"

Mholda, a taller than average man with a thinner than average body build, he has not been eating well. His clothes are hanging from his body like they do on a branch. Although there are a lot of layers to fight the cold, it is obvious they used to fit him better. He might have passed as a handsome man in his youth, there's not a drop of color left in his clothes, nor his face. Mholda used to be a friendly person, but a visual inspection today would make one wonder the exact opposite. He is an outsider, a loner, a drifter - a man who has nothing and belongs to nowhere.

"There you are, you prick," he mutters to himself as a squirrel with a whole white tail and purple feet stares at him from a tree branch, eating a berry.

The squirrel has been following him from day one in the woods. Squirrels in the woods are nothing special, but a squirrel with a white tail is considered sacred in the culture. They lead the people towards a wealth meant for kings. But this particular squirrel has changed camps with Mholda, he's been following him from treetop to treetop, hiding away at night only to come out as soon as Mholda starts moving.

While Mholda has never been a great hunter he has learned some tricks while living in exile. But his main diet is still berries and an occasional bird eggs.

Mholda stares at the squirrel eating the berry, then looks at his purple feet, Mholda connects the dots and looks towards his cave. There's a willow leaf covered in crushed berries.

"Oh you crossed the line now,"

The thought of what to do is clear,

"It's been a long time since I had a nice meal, some berries, smoke you in birch, mmm,"

The squirrel is at a man's height, but too far to reach.

"I can make it, I will make it. You're done," Mholda keeps his eyes on the squirrel, he kneels down and drags his hand through the ground for something he can pick up. His hands touch a pebble, he picks it up. He will not hit the squirrel, it's far too small. Mholda flicks the pebble with his thumb, it goes over the squirrel and lands on the rock, the squirrel turns. Mholda starts sprinting as fast as his legs can carry. He steps from rock to rock, without looking at his feet - his eyes are on the prize. The squirrel turns just in time to see Mholda's hands around it. The joy of catching something with his bare hands makes him scream from the top of his lungs. He laughs out loud.

"I am the better man!"

Mholda looks at the squirrel which drains all of his excitement.

"Why are you not struggling? I won,"

The squirrel is motionless between his two big bony hands. He can feel the branch under his armpits, cutting right to his bone. Mholda tries to find footing with his legs, but there's nothing. He looks down and sees a big sloped drop that would end him.

"You sneaky fucker," Mholda is hanging on the tree by his armpits, still holding on to the squirrel. There's barely any muscle on his arms, he can feel the tree bark cutting into his bone. The squirrel seems to be laughing. Mholda keeps a straight face and tightens his grip on the squirrel - no reaction. He tightens the grip to a point where his fingers start hurting - no reaction. He can't do it.

"Who are you?" Mholda lets the squirrel go, it climbs on his left arm, back into the tree.

Now that the squirrel is gone, pain in the arms grows exponentially, he lets one of his arms down and grabs the branch with his hand. Almost immediately the other one follows - he's weak. Mholda stretches out his toes, trying to grab the ledge behind him, the dirt crumbles and rolls down the ledge. Mholda looks up into the sky, the squirrel jumps from a branch in front of him to behind him.

He tries to lift his left arm to get a better grip, it slips back down. He starts swinging his legs to gather momentum.

"One… two….. Three… fuck!," he let's go, legs slip underneath him and falls on his ass - it's on the ledge. He quickly rolls away from it, lying on his back. The squirrel is eating another berry.

Mholda stops at a cliff and sees a village by the fjord, people are moving, a fishing boat returning.

He walks towards a house with a deer carcass on his shoulder and axe in hand. Not a single soul is walking the village, the chicken coup is empty, the boat he had seen from the cliff is not in harbour, no kids running around, an eerie quiet at this time of the year.

He looks for dogs but sees none, drops the deer in front of a well kept house and pushes the door open. He can hear rustling in the back and follows the noise.

"I caught a deer,"

No reply, behind the fireplace he sees a man on his bed, on top of his wife. They are uninterrupted by Mholda. He draws the axe, it lands right in the spine. The man falls on the bed without any sound. He can feel the blood coming to his fingers - this was the first time Mholda had killed a man - there's a faint smile.

"Carl," the recluse boat builder who lives by himself, just to avoid conflict.

Mholda opens his eyes, a tear runs down his cheek.

The strong current of the river is gushing through, a moose with antlers the size of Mholda is scratching himself on a tree across the river. Mholda is sitting on a rock, thinking about the incident that got him banished from the village. Village where he grew up and became a man, where he first lay with a woman.

The thought of banishment feels different today. Mholda feels empty, directionless.

"Where do I have to go?" it has always been about survival, then it became about catching the squirrel, "I got you," he mutters to the river.

"Where are you?"

The squirrel jumps on the branch Mholda was directly looking at.

"I always wondered how long can you keep up, when will you come say hi. It might not have been most viking like with conquering, sex and glory but I guess it was romantic"

Mholda had been traveling around for a long time since he was banished from the village, walking from one river to the next sleeping in caves, slits and trees until he came across a seemingly cozy cave which he thought was suitable for living, there was nice natural protection, a wall to reflect heat of a fire from and it was big enough to stand without hitting his head. A river flowing right beside meant constant food source and most important of all, it was in deep woods with no one else around.

"You know, I tried catching you the first months. But I could never bring myself to kill you. Maybe that's why you kept away - you knew. Did you?" Mholda is expecting a reply from the squirrel, who licks it's hands and rubs them on it's face.

"You knew," Mholda says with confidence. "But when I fried that fish, I swear to Odin, you knew I was a friend and would not hurt you."

The sun is behind the trees, light is falling in the forest, but the river is still flowing. Mholda is on the same rock, looking at the river, his stomach rumbles. He wants to be home next to his wife in the sheep skin bed, not in a cave, on a rock covered with moss with an unintelligent squirrel.

He's been working on ideas for the past days, the cave becomes stranger and more uncomfortable by the day.

It is clear that he can't just walk back and hope he's forgiven. There is an execution on spot order on him and vikings love killing, if they can do it legally, even little children trying to prove they are old enough for a raid will try to cut him down.

Viking folklore is full of stories of the past conquerors, the gods and the myths. Mholda's grandmother had an infinite amount of stories to tell but there was always one story that was repeated and everyone knew by heart. The Draug who lives on the forbidden hill, guarding the treasure from men. No one knows what the treasure is but they all agree, it is worthy of kings - this might just do it. But finding it would prove difficult. The Draug is cursed and the land around him smears from his aura. It drives the men mad just as good as it does animals. Even sheep don't go eating there. Mholda heard stories of sheep who were driven so mad, they had started eating their own wool and choked to death, of men, who wanted treasure and glory, but never returned, countless of them. While the start of those stories is different, the end is always certain, you don't go on telling the story yourself, for dead men tell no tales. But if there is a way to get back into the village, Mholda has to take the chance. All the riches he would bring to the village might be enough to rally the villagers behind him for a pardon.

Everything Mholda knows about Draugs comes from stories his father's mother told him when he was not even old enough to catch chickens. To defeat a Draug, one needs to have willpower, strength and cunningness. Draugs are always stronger than their opponent with a power to change it's size from a field mouse to a great ox. They can sit flat on your chest until you stop breathing or will climb into your lungs and chew their way out through your chest.

Finding a Draug would be the easy part - time is everything Mholda has. Wandering around the forest until he finds a hill where no animal dares to go should not be difficult. Specially if it smells like a mass grave after a great disease. It might be that their own body is decaying or their very presence is just so awful, living nature can't endure it and starts rotting just to end it's own misery.

Something that makes Mholda worried are good reflexes which he is sure to need if he wants to meet a Draug and come back alive. Draugs are known to come through solid materials like a mist and appear in front of you within a blink of an eye.

"So many days and you still haven't thought of everything, stupid," he stares at his old axe that had been in Carl's back. There are faint smudges of blood on it. He picks up the axe and leaves the riverside.

"Ok, so I'm going to sneak in with a torch," he picks up a burning stick, "and light the whole grave on fire, get out and wait for him to burn,"

The squirrel looks back at him in wonder. "Here," Mholda gives the squirrel a blueberry.

"But that would destroy the treasure…" Mholda sits on the ground with disappointment.

"Do you know Turan?" he stands up and starts pacing in front of the squirrel.

"Turan was an ancient viking king, who was usurped by his two sons. They cast him out and he want straight on a path to find and kill a Draug to prove himself. But he was not only strong, but cunning as well. Turan covered his sword in sap and lit it on fire. When Draug came out of his grave, Turan slashed him with his sword, the fire cut the Draug who screamed so loud, all the animals ran away from his old village. Everyone knew what he was doing then. But the screaming stopped as suddenly as it had started. Turan stood with the Draug's head on the ground, in front of him," Mholda kneels and picks up a burning log to imitate a sword.

"We're going home"

Sun is just about to rise. Mholda is packing his camp which means grabbing a few berries, an axe and birch bark to make a quick fire. He rustles up the remains of the fire and set on his way with axe in hand. There's no way of knowing where the Draug might be but he knows, it's near a river so he decides to follow the river down as vikings usually live by the coast for convenient transportation.

As soon as he stepped his first step, his stomach started a gurgle that berries alone won't stop.

"Alright, one last time," By the river he found his tangled rod and used some of the berries he had collected. On the same rock, he decided to embark on the final adventure he cast his line. All he now has to do was wait. Staring into the water gave Mholda some time to think.

"What if the draug has a battleaxe?"

He looks around the area and notices a thin stone, one storm away from breaking off to a solo adventure. As he walks closer, the stone is a lot bigger than previously.

"I can't attach a handle to this anyway,"

Three man's length in front of him is fallen tree, that stretches over the river. "This wasn't here yesterday,"

A perfect tree with only four branches on the other bank. Perfect for a shield. He starts sculpting one of the roots the size of a man. His old axe barely goes through the root which gives him more hope.

"That's definitely more than two blows," he hacks vigorously until the root drops.

Mholda picks up a one piece cylindrical shield and ducks behind it. None of his body is visible.

"I am a natural," He is extremely pleased with himself.

Walking back to the rod he exercises with the shield and the axe, turning, ducking, swinging blows. He notices his rod on the ground, something has pulled it. Mholda switches into a sprint to get to the rod in time, throws his fresh shield and axe on the rocks and leaps to the rod, catching it in water. If this is a fish, it will be the smallest catch of spring. He gets on his feet and pulls out an empty hook. In a burst of anger he throws the rod into the river, the hook catches his pants. This makes Mholda so angry, he sits down from disappointment.

"We're not past the first rock and you're already giving up?," he says to himself,

"Use the line, throw away the rod," he tries to talk sense into himself.

He pulls in the line, detaches it from the stick and pockets the line. He let's out a big sigh as in what to do now. He starts walking downstream, picking berries and sour apples from a tree by the river.

"You have probably fed generations, if not dozens before me, stay safe old man," he pats the tree and walks away with a cloth sack full of apples, an axe on his back and a massive shield in hand.

"I never liked the apples," Mholda throws away a half eaten apple. He chews the last piece of it and makes a face - sour. He climbs down to the riverside and takes a sip of water by dunking his head in. It's cold and refreshing, helps to keep his head clear. As his head is dripping water back into the river he opens his eyes and notices a bird flying into an old maple tree. That means either eggs or babies. Mholda would prefer eggs, there's barely any meat on the chicks and he does not want to build a fire.

He leaves his shield on the ground and starts climbing the old Maple. It's not difficult, there's always a new branch to put your leg to. As he gets closer to the top, two birds evacuate the tree,Mholda keeps climbing.

"Why do I even try," The nest is empty, he topples it from the branch and sits on it himself. It's the tallest maple in the area, almost as high as pines. He can faintly see over the trees. Mholda notices something.

He climbs even higher to a point where the branches are so young, they can barely hold a swallow. A branch breaks underneath Mholda's left foot, he has his eyes set on the prize.

"The Draug,"

A hill with a massive dead tree one day's walk down the river.

Mholda's feet touch the soil with a loud thump. He picks up his shield and starts walking directly towards the hill.

"I have to make it," Mholda is panting, pushing himself through the thickening vegetation. The woods have changed from a green lush vegetation to forest where not even a soul seems to live. The trees have no bark, just lines of old dark red sap running down the trunk.

Mholda stopped to gather his breath. He can see the sun set behind the trees. "Finally," he grabbed his axe and started chopping the thinner branches that are sharp enough to leave deep cuts on Mholda's face. He looks as if he's fought a black bear.

A trail of branches follows Mholda, he is not picking the easiest route, he is hacking through the forest in a straight line as to separate his land from everyone else's.

An axe comes through the branches, it is followed by a man who chopped through a thick forest but looks like he took a light stroll in the woods. He takes a minute to look at where he arrived.

"Hmmm.." The forest looks like an exact copy of the forest he came from. Pine trees, maples, a river but not a single drop of life or a sound, even the rustling river is quiet.

"Better rest up, big fight coming," Mholda walks towards the river, looking for a hidden cave between river rocks. During his time in the wilderness, he has gotten accustomed to sleeping in caves. Although he does not enjoy it, sleeping out in the open is worse.

Mholda kneels beside the river, drinks the water. He swings his head from right to left, grimaces and swallows. Foul taste resembling the time Mholda found a deer carcass upstream, halfway in the river. He looks downstream with some whitewater and upstream with fast flowing water but the river makes the noise of a small stream.

The sun has set and Mholda has found no caves. The only option left - gather sticks.

He starts gathering longer sticks to make shelter under a fallen pine tree.

"You better not fall on me again," says Mholda while laying sticks to one side of the tree. He picks moss from the rocks by the river, taking off big chunks at a time and lays them underneath the fallen tree. He throws sticks on top and lays down.

With his heavy shield on top of him to shelter from elements and trap his own bodyheat, Mholda laid under the tree. He can't close his eyes. It might be the anxiety of the upcoming fight, it might be the cold or it might be the forest. He thought it better to not make a fire and preserve the energy for the fight. It might also attract the Draug's attention and Mholda wants to keep the element of surprise.

"Draug, Draug, Draug, Draug,"

His makeshift shelter is bursting up in flames along with the shield. Mholda laying underneath it, he can't move. There's a figure on top of him which he can't make it out clear enough to identify. Yellow light flickering on his face, but Mholda's jaw is rattling like a woodpecker looking for termites. The figure comes closer, it's not bending, it's hovering. Mholda can feel the ice cold breath - blueberries.

"Murder," a faint voice echos in Mholda's ears with a gushing river. Mholda stares at the black fog on top of him, trying to understand who it is. His jaw still rattling, the figure is gone in a blink. Mholda rolls from underneath the shelter and is up in a heartbeat. He looks around to see the figure - it's too dark to make anything out.

A crack. Mholda turns to the sound - someone stepped on a branch. He grabs his axe, looking directly at the sound. Noises in the forest are nothing special. They usually turn out to be harmless animals wandering around, but Mholda was certain this is the time when it's not a fox or a boar. It's a bear, or the Draug.

Another branch. Mholda looks to the right, upriver. Bear's stomp, you can feel the step of a bear, this was something else.

"Heeeeey!" Mholda starts making noise in hopes to scare the unknown monster away.

"I've got an axe!" the steps keep coming closer. Mholda backs slowly.

"I'll cut you." He's lost the confidence in his voice.

"Don't make me do it," he can barely see his shelter anymore from which a loud crack comes. Mholda looks at the axe in his hands and reaches to the back - nothing.

"My shield," he backs into a massive oak tree, tightens his grip on the axe, the steps keep coming closer. Mholda squints his eyes to see in the dark, another branch breaks in front of him. The creature is right on the edge of darkness. Mholda can make out a figure. Unlike his dream, he knows what this is.

The warm breath of the figure steams in the air. The deer steps closer. Mholda is confused. Usually it was the deer running as soon as they heard Mholda in the area. But something is off with this deer.

"Draug," as soon as the words come from his mouth, the deer charges. Mholda backs himself behind the oak. The deer follows which makes Mholda run a lap around the oak. He jumps behind a massive ground root, stretches his hands and legs so he is completely hidden behind the root. The deer jumps over him. Mholda gets up and makes his way into the forest, he can see the deer charging over the shoulder. He hides behind a tree that has his shoulders sticking out from both side of the tree. He turns around.

"Fucking goat, I will eat you!" this could be the best meal Mholda has had in a while. The last time he licked his fingers after a meal was when he found a cuckoo walking around and smacked him in the head. But he could be the one getting smacked on the head now. No deer was ever this violent.

The deer slowed it's pace, walking towards Mholda. It stops two body lengths away from him.

All the thoughts of eating the deer went right out the window. It breathes like a raging river, it's never taken it's eyes off Mholda - the eyes were plain white like the winter's snow.

"It's real," he told the deer, but meaning it more to himself. "You've seen him, you met him. She was right. Animals go crazy there. So it must be around here, right?" all Mholda can hear is the deer breathing.

The two stare at each other. Mholda's scared look has been replaced with determination. He now has the confirmation that the Draug's treasure is real. Getting mauled by a deer might be the easiest battle he has to face, so he will face it.

Mholda blinks, the two stare at each other. He steps out from behind the tree, he blinks again. He lets out a wild scream, deer doesn't flinch. He blinks. Mholda's breaths get longer. Another blink. He grabs the axe as tight as he can. The deer exhales and takes a step forward. Mholda takes an accidental step back. The deer has the upper hand now. It leaps towards Mholda who trips over fallen tree. While falling he can see a white line of fur under the deer's belly. It's hind legs land right behind Mholda's head, just enough to scrape the hair.

Mholda sits up, looking for his axe. He stumbles across the log, picks it up and stands as tall as possible.

"Come get it" he yells into the empty forest with no sign of the deer, not even steps are heard.

As he walks back to his camp, he can't stop thinking about the deer. Did it run back to the Draug or did it come from the Draug. Either way Mholda has to investigate. But if he reacted like this to wildlife, how will he react when the Draug from behind the grave shows up?

As he got back to the camp, he saw his shield on the ground in two pieces.

"You motherf…" the loud crack he had heard before was the shield snapping in two under the deer's hoof. Mholda picks up the side with the handle, it is terribly unbalanced. He can't get the axe in his other hand, he needs both hands to support the shield, he throws it on his back. It doesn't look good, nor feels comfortable but he reckons, it might come in handy.

Sleep was off the table. After a restless night and a meeting with a crazed deer, there was no chance he could even close his eyes and think of resting. Might as well get an early start and find the Draug.

Mholda decided to keep the shelter, someone might need it one day, unlikely, but someone might. He decides to make his way down the river to get a sip, a foul sip, but the body requires water, specially in this habitat. He walked downstream from where he had the water earlier until he found another spot with good access to river from man sized rocks. The rocks were slippery, they get covered during flood and a slime like substance covers them. Carefully testing each rock with his left leg before putting his whole body onto it, Mholda is making his way down. He is right at the bottom, when his leg slips and he falls on his back. Mholda's legs are in the water, getting carried along the stream, but the shield on his back is lodged between two rocks. He pushes himself up with his legs, but the bottom rock is too slippery. The shield is secured well. He puts his hands over his head and pulls from the shield. The body moves up, but the shield dislodges and Mholda falls down. He falls in a sitting position on the slippery rock with legs in the water. The stream is so powerful, his legs float on the surface. He feels secure and washes his face sitting on the rock. Mholda take's a look around to inspect the situation.

Both sides of the riverbank are filled with trees. The left side is black trees without leaves, the right bank is flourishing with birds on the branches. Looking ahead he sees no way to cross it.

Mholda pulls his legs in, trying to turn around on the rock. He lays down on his left thigh, putting both knees on the rock. Just above him are the two rocks his shield was wedged between, the only way up.

He stands up like a deer on a frozen lake, but his up. Bending over to touch the two rocks, he jumps. He's on the rock like moss, but besides his hands and friction, there is nothing holding him, the legs have no support. He presses his forearms on the rock and lifts his behind, he moves up a little.

"Like a frog humping a rock," he murmurs to himself angrily. He does it again, more progress.

"A true Draug slayer,", more progress.

"Humping a rock for a warm up," more progress.

He continues until he is on the rock, standing up with disappointment in his eyes. The failure beside river has given him thoughts of quitting. A sudden roar breaks the silence. He looks on the other riverbank. A bear has been following his escapades from the other side of the river. It nods to him and walks away.

"A sign" he murmurs to himself. Mholda starts putting distance between himself and the river.

The forest is just thick enough to make navigation difficult. The sun is rising, but which way from the hill it rises from? There's no sound from the river and he does not know what river this is so where does it flow? South or West? It is now all up to blind luck.

The sun was at the day's highest when Mholda reached a clearance but there was no hill. "Is this the same clearance? But there was only one"

He slowed his pace and walked on the clearance, taking the surroundings in. Lush green birch trees on the sides, even on the side he just came from.

"What the… I just came through here, this was all dead." He murmus to himself, finding it hard to believe. A rabbit is sitting on the edge of the forest, sniffing at something. He looks to the left and runs away. A deer is eating by itself. Mholda freezes. His last interaction with a deer had not gone well. He feels for the axe on his side. The deer looks at frozen Mholda, trying to figure out what moved, it's looking straight at him but lowers his head to keep eating.

"I got you now," Mholda unsheaths his axe, slowly starting to move. The deer is alert, raises it's head once again, looking at Mholda. The two look at each other, it darts into the forest.

Mholda straightens himself, leaves the axe in his hand and starts walking to the other side of the clearance with a massive grey birch tree. As he gets closer, he notices a sketching on a tree. Scars on the tree has straight lines. Someone has carved it years before.

"M and… H?" he inspects it further finding more lines which are indecipherable. "MH?" It dawns on him, "Mholda! He's waiting for me. He must be close," Mholda leaves the tree and follows the forest after it, which turns out to be a thin strip of vegetation leading into another clearing. This one with a hill.

"The Draug"

Mholda drops everything besides his axe and his half beaten up shield, which is still strapped to his back with sides of shield hanging out from either side of him.

With coldness in the air, Mholda makes his way towards the hill. Although it's not a big trek, it takes time as his steps get slower and smaller after each one with his heart rate going up with elevation. A single stone lies on top of the hill. Mholda notices the writing on it. Now there was no doubt, this was the home of the Draug.

Magnus, never has there been mightier or fiercer god.

"A god?" his axe is knocked out of his hand. Mholda does not even start looking for it. The Draug is right in front of him.

Extremely thin long hair, plain white eyes, ripped shirt with ribs showing underneath it. Three long nails on his right arm, only bones on his left arm. Boots from two centuries ago with leather barely holding together. And the stench. If you weren't looking at it, you'd think there had been a plague with bodies right behind the corner.

All of the ravens from the nearby trees took off. With his head turned, he was suddenly on his back with an undead King towering above him.

"Mholda, the mighty Draug slayer," he second guesses himself. Mholda can't bear to look the Draug in it's eyes, he diverts his eyes down, looking at the Draug's feet. It has untorn bearskin pants that do not fit the tattered look of the Draug. While looking at the bear fur he notices his axe from the left corner of his eye. With nothing to lose, he kicks the Draug in it's shin and rolls left to grab the axe.

He grabs the axe, is up in a heartbeat just to see the Draug land face first onto the exact same patch of grass he was lying on the second before. It is getting up, without a thought Mholda plants his axe in it's back, only to fall short, sticking the axe in the ground in front of him. The Draug is up, Mholda backs two steps, the Draug steps on his axe, becoming one with the ground without a handle to be seen.

"Last chance," he thought. Grabbing the shield from his back.

"Come get it!" Mholda screams. The Draug rushes him. A force Mholda has not experienced before hits his shield, the shield recoils into his head, the wooden shield is blown into pieces, Mholda falls on his back. With a dizzy head, he gets up without thinking what might come next. His head is spinning, turning everywhere, Draug is nowhere. Mholda notices two viking warriors who must have heard the commotion.

"Grab your swords! The Draug is here!" expecting them to rush to help, the vikings stopped and looked at each other. They nodded and sprinted towards him.

Mholda looks around for the Draug when he notices a brown dug up patch in the ground. He pokes it with his leg.

"I am not going anywhere"

"Come out or I'll dig you out,"

Mholda feels a force from his back, he lands face first into the dirt. His hands are forced behind his back and bound up.

The next day a newspaper with an article about Mholda appears along with a photo of him.

"Mailman killer caught living in wild"

Printed in Great Britain
by Amazon